3

Little Penguin and Baby Seal
got a sled.

They pulled the sled
up a big hill.

The Sledding Adventure

Written by Michèle Dufresne
Illustrated by Cula Carmen Elena

Contents

The Sledding Adventure   2

The Sledding Adventure: The Play   14

Polar Bears   18

PIONEER VALLEY EDUCATIONAL PRESS, INC.

The Sledding Adventure

"Come on!"
called Little Penguin.
"Let's go sledding."

"OK," said Baby Seal.

Little Penguin and Baby Seal
went down the big hill
on the sled.

"Whee!" said Little Penguin.

"Whee!" said Baby Seal.

"Let's go down
the hill again!"
said Little Penguin.

Little Penguin and Baby Seal
pulled the sled back up the hill.

They got onto the sled
and went down the hill again.

Little Penguin and Baby Seal went down, down, down the hill.

The sled went faster and faster.

"Oh, no!"
said Little Penguin.
"We are going
into the sea!"

"Uh-oh," said Baby Seal.

"Help! Help!"
cried Little Penguin
and Baby Seal.

"Oh, no!"
said Mrs. Polar Bear.
"Little Penguin and Baby Seal
are in the sea!"

"They are in the sea again?"
asked Grandpa Walrus.
He shook his head.

Mrs. Polar Bear
and Grandpa Walrus swam
out to get Little Penguin
and Baby Seal.

They pulled Little Penguin,
Baby Seal, and the sled
back to shore.

"Thank you!"
said Little Penguin.

"Thank you!" said Baby Seal.

The Sledding Adventure: The Play

Come on!
Let's go sledding.

OK!
Let's go sledding!

Little Penguin
and Baby Seal
got a sled. They
pulled the sled
up a big hill.

Little Penguin
and Baby Seal
went down the hill.

Whee!

Oh, no!
We are going into
the sea!

Uh-oh!

Oh, no!
Help! Help! Help!

Help! Help! Help!

Oh, no!
Little Penguin and
Baby Seal are
in the sea.

They are in the sea
again?

Grandpa Walrus and Mrs. Polar Bear went into the sea to get Little Penguin and Baby Seal.

Thank you!

Thank you!

Polar Bears

Polar bears live where it is cold. They like to hunt on the ice. They hunt seals, fish, and small whales. Polar bears have white fur. They are white like the snow and ice.

Polar bears are good
at swimming. They swim
in the cold water.

In the winter, a mother polar bear stays in a den. Baby polar bears are called cubs. They are born in the den.

In the spring, the mother polar bear and her cub come out of the den. They are very hungry!